AF067521

PROMISE ME

Titles in Between The Lines:

HOPE AND TRUTH
DANIEL BLYTHE

KISS THE SKY
DANIEL BLYTHE

REFUGEE KID
CATHERINE BRUTON

ANNIE
TOMMY DONBAVAND

PROMISE ME
ANN EVANS

SILENT VALLEY
CLIFF McNISH

MADE
KATE ORMAND

SIREN SONG
JACQUELINE RAYNER

Badger Publishing Limited, Oldmedow Road, Hardwick Industrial Estate, King's Lynn PE30 4JJ

Telephone: 01438 791037

www.badgerlearning.co.uk

PROMISE ME

ANN EVANS

Promise Me ISBN 978-1-78837-212-1

Text © Ann Evans 2017
Complete work © Badger Publishing Limited 2017

All rights reserved. No part of this publication may be reproduced, stored in any form or by any means mechanical, electronic, recording or otherwise without the prior permission of the publisher.

The right of Ann Evans to be identified as author of this Work has been asserted by her in accordance with the Copyright, Designs and Patents Act 1988.

Publisher: Susan Ross
Senior Editor: Danny Pearson
Editorial Coordinator: Claire Morgan
Copyeditor: Cambridge Publishing Management
Designer: Bigtop Design Ltd
Cover: © Tetra Images / Alamy Stock Photo

6 8 10 9 7 5

CHAPTER 1
THE BOY NEXT DOOR

He arrived in the night — Amos. That should have told me. Warned me.

Amos — an unusual name for an unusual boy. That's what he said anyway. Only then, I hadn't known just how unusual.

Nor had I known that he would break my heart. Break it into a million pieces.

And I would break his.

*

It was the start of the long summer holidays. I woke to hear voices coming from next door. Things being banged about. Furniture being moved. Those sort of noises.

So at last, someone had moved in next door. The house had stood empty for ages.

I was dying to know who our new neighbours were.

I *really hoped* it would be some fit guy.

I didn't actually expect it to be. That was my normal daydream. They say I'm a dreamer, a romantic.

But what's wrong with that?

I'm not such a dreamer that I don't do my school work. Just the opposite. My emotions and dreams are reflected in my artwork and my English. I write poetry and love stories. I paint in pastel colours, kind of like Monet. Sort of hazy, romantic colours — beautiful people, beautiful places, beautiful things.

Kids at school tease me loads.

"Get real, Lisa," my best mate Nina is always saying. "You watch too many soppy films."

But that morning, back at the start of the summer holidays, was the start of a new dream.

How was I to know it would turn into a nightmare?

"Mum! New people have moved in."

She was dashing about as usual, getting ready for work. "Yes, so it seems."

"Have you met them?" I asked.

She gave me one of her looks. "Lisa, they've only just got here. They must have moved in very early this morning, or late last night."

"Or in the dead of night," I added.

She slid the cereal and fruit juice my way. "Anyway, are you going to be OK on your own all day, with your dad and me at work?"

"I'm not a baby, Mum."

I was already making plans. I'd heard a young guy's voice through our paper-thin walls. And an older couple's voices. So a teenager and his parents. So far so good.

Once Mum had set off for work, I nipped upstairs, showered, washed my hair. Sat in front of my mirror, drying it.

I have long, black hair and brown eyes. I'm just ordinary really. But today I didn't want to look ordinary. I wanted to look drop-dead gorgeous for when the guy next door set eyes on me.

I truly believe in love at first sight. And if he was fit, then I wanted to give myself the best chance of making him fall for me.

I put my make-up on really carefully. My eyes are quite large and almond shaped. With mascara and eyeliner and a smoky grey eyeshadow, they look pretty good. Nina says they look *stunning*.

That's the effect I wanted to have on him.

I wanted to stun him!

It was odd hearing people moving about next door. And I know it was a bit wicked, but I put my ear against the wall and listened….

"So where's your desk and laptop going?"

"By the window please, Dad."

"Keyboard?"

"Right there would be good."

I smiled to myself. He sounded nice — cheerful, not moody like most of the lads in my class. And his bedroom, like mine, looked out over the back garden.

It was another hot day, so I wore denim shorts and a loose top. I checked how I looked in the mirror — back view, front view. Not bad!

A quick spray of perfume. It was a lovely floaty scent, dreamy. Nina had got it me for Christmas. She said it matched my personality.

Now, I didn't want to look obvious. You know, hanging about in the garden, hoping to catch sight of him. I'm not that sad. So I took my artist's easel outside.

I was doing some watercolour paintings for a school project. The topic was nature. And our garden was full of flowers, birds, bees and butterflies.

I put the easel and my chair in the middle of the lawn. There was a low fence between the gardens. Standing, I could see next door's house clearly. Their back door and windows were open, blowing the cobwebs out, I guess.

His bedroom window had the curtains shut. But music was drifting out. I liked his choice of music.

I began my painting. First, sketching the outline of some roses, then mixing red and white on my pallet to get just the right shades of pink. With the music and the sun shining, I kind of got lost in my work.

Before I knew it, it was lunchtime — and I hadn't even glimpsed him.

A bit disappointed, I went indoors.

CHAPTER 2
DREAMING

Over the next few days it started to bug me. I saw his parents. They went in and out of the house and garden. They smiled and said hello. But no sign of the guy.

Lying in bed reading one night, I heard someone singing and playing piano — *keyboard*! Of course, his dad had asked where the keyboard should go.

Wow! So he played keyboard and sang. This was getting better and better!

He was good enough to be on *The X Factor* or *Britain's Got Talent*. And as I lay in bed listening to him singing his songs, I dreamed he was singing just for me.

Later in the week, I saw his mum and dad going out in their car. He wasn't with them. So, I made sure I was looking my best, this time in a floaty top with my hair clipped up. The curls that hung around my face had taken half an hour to get right.

I set up my easel and chair. The painting was coming along well. I tried not to glance too much at his house. I saw that today all the windows and the back door were open to let the fresh air blow through, but the curtains and kitchen blinds were shut. There was even a bead curtain in the back doorway so you couldn't see into the kitchen.

I was starting to think someone liked the dark.

I was busy painting when he started to sing. He must have been in the kitchen, and his voice rang out across the gardens. It sent goosebumps up and down my arms.

I couldn't help myself. When he'd finished, I clapped and called out, "Hey! That was really good!"

The silence that followed went on forever.

And then, a boy's voice said, "Thanks."

I put my paintbrush down and went over to the fence. "You have a great voice. You should be on *The X Factor*."

"Ha! I don't think so."

I waited for him to come out. But he stayed inside.

"I'm Lisa, by the way."

Silence.

I kept my smile firmly in place. "So, what's your name? Seeing as we're neighbours."

"Me? I'm Amos."

"Amos? That's unusual."

"Yep, that's me. An unusual name for an unusual guy."

I was starting to think he *was* unusual. Any normal person would at least have popped their head out to say hello.

"So what's so unusual about you?" I asked.

"Oh, this and that."

"You've got two heads, have you?"

He laughed again. It was a nice sound. It sent a little tremor up my spine.

"No, three!"

"Well one of them has a really nice singing voice," I joked. "I heard you the other night in your room. My bedroom is next to yours. Do you write your own music and lyrics?"

He sounded a bit worried. "I hope it didn't bother you. I could get my dad to soundproof my walls…"

"Don't you dare!" I laughed. "I like it!"

Then I blushed. *Cool it*, I warned myself.

We chatted about music then. I talked about my favourite singers and bands, and he did too. Most of the ones he liked I'd never heard of, but he talked so passionately about them, I knew I'd be looking them up on YouTube later.

But it was the weirdest conversation ever.

He must have had a clear view of me, standing out in the sunshine, but I couldn't see him at all. So finally, I said, "It would be nice to see you. Can't you pop out? Just so I can check you don't have three heads!"

He laughed again. "No, sorry. I never go out."

The word *never* hit me like a brick.

"You never go out? What about school?"

"Home-schooled."

"What about keeping fit? Fresh air is good for you, you know!"

"I'm fine," he said.

"But what about friends? You need friends!"

For the first time, I heard sadness in his voice. "Friends let you down."

"Not always," I said, thinking how Nina and I had been best mates forever.

"Yes they do."

His words sounded so final, so true, that a sharp pain jabbed at my heart.

CHAPTER 3
COME OUTSIDE — PLEASE

We chatted over the garden fence most days. I gave up asking him to come outside. He clearly had a fear of open spaces.

"So what are you painting?" he asked, one afternoon.

I put my hands on my hips. "Why not come and see for yourself?"

The silence rang in my ears.

I ran to the fence. "Amos… Amos?"

I felt sick. Maybe he *couldn't* come out. Maybe he was disabled. In a wheelchair or bed-ridden. I felt awful for pushing him, making a joke out of his problem. Whatever it was.

"Amos!"

He sounded so sad when he spoke. "It's OK. I'm guessing you're painting the roses. I can imagine you're good. I don't need to see it."

Tears pricked my eyes as I picked up my painting. Took it back to the fence so he could see it.

I held it out until my arms ached.

I was starting to think he'd gone off into another room.

But then he said, "That is amazing! Beautiful!"

I was so relieved to hear his voice again I wanted to cry. I bit my lip. "Thank you."

"A beautiful painting, by a beautiful girl."

Oh! My knees went weak.

I didn't know what to say. So I muttered another "Thank you."

I felt a bit lost then. Should I go indoors? Carry on with my painting? What I wanted was to be close to him. To see him. It didn't matter if he was afraid of the outdoors.

I wanted to touch his hand. To show him I would never let him down. That it was nothing to be afraid of.

"Lisa…."

His voice startled me. "Yes, Amos?"

"I was thinking. We should swap mobile numbers and emails. The weather won't always be this nice. Can't have you standing out in the rain and snow, talking to this weirdo!"

"You're not a weirdo!"

"Oh, I am, Lisa. Take my word for it," he replied.

"Well, maybe I like weirdos!"

"You'll find there are limits. Anyway, what's your mobile number? I'll text you my email address. Then we'll be able to stay in touch, in all weathers."

I couldn't believe winter would be here before I set eyes on Amos. I *had* to see him before then. This was crazy.

But I told him my number, and when I checked my phone later, he'd texted me his email address. I sent him an email. His reply came back in seconds.

Later that evening, he rang me. I hadn't expected a call. I took my mobile up to my room. It felt so intimate hearing his voice in my bedroom. I curled up on my bed, hugging the phone close.

"Just thought I'd bug you!" he said. "What are you up to?"

"Just watching TV. How about you?"

"Working on the laptop. I'm a computer geek, you know."

There was laughter in his voice. And I could hear him talking faintly, through the wall.

"That's handy to know," I said, closing my eyes. Picturing him at his laptop by the window. "What do you do?"

"My plan is to be a professional geek!" He laughed again. "No, actually I plan on being a website designer and programmer. I've got a few clients already.... Building up my empire!"

My heart sank. The perfect job. He'd never have to leave the house.

"Sounds good," I said, not really meaning it.

"I'm hoping so. I'm doing online courses. Getting my qualifications."

We chatted on. Not just about him. He wanted to know all about me. My plans for the future. He was easy to talk to. He made me laugh.

But sometimes, secretly, he made me cry.

Nina decided he was, for sure, a weirdo!

"Don't go falling for him, Lisa!" she said, as we walked home from school. It was late September, and I still hadn't set eyes on him.

"I won't," I lied.

She shot me a knowing look. "Oh, Lisa, you idiot! You already have, haven't you?"

I shrugged. "Well, maybe a little bit."

She groaned. "Don't do this! What's the point? You can't go out together. Falling for him means you won't fall for any *normal* lad."

"Maybe I don't want a normal lad."

I avoided her eyes. She knew I was lying. I *did* want a normal boyfriend. Someone to go out with. Have fun with. See places together. Go to parties, the cinema. I longed just to go walking hand in hand with the boy I loved.

I dreamed of love — one day.

I dreamed of being with Amos.

CHAPTER 4
A PHOTO OF YOU

That evening, I rang him. His cheery voice made me feel good.

"I was just going to ring you!" he said.

I curled up on my bed. "Great minds think alike."

We chatted about our day, and what we'd been doing. He was building a website which sounded very complicated. Clearly he was a genius!

And he always liked to hear about my school life, about Nina.

"I bet she thinks I'm a right weirdo," he said, sounding amused. "Bet she tells you to have nothing to do with me."

"Yes, something like that."

"Can't blame her."

"She wants to know why you won't go out," I said, longing to understand his problem.

"Tell Nina I don't want to scare the neighbours," he joked.

"So why would they be scared?" I kept my voice light. "I know… you're a vampire!"

He laughed. "I'd be a rubbish one. I go queasy at the sight of blood."

"So are you a little short for your age?"

"Let's not get personal!"

"You're a giant, then?"

"Fee-fi-fo-fum, I smell the blood of an Englishman…. Yeuk! Feel sick!"

"Seriously," I asked. "Are you in a wheelchair, Amos, because…"

"No, I'm not in a wheelchair."

"OK… so have you got *three* heads?"

He sighed. "OK, you've got it. I'm a three-headed monster."

I could tell he was getting bored with my questions. I knew his problem. It was mental. He had a phobia.

Maybe he couldn't admit it to himself. And nagging him wasn't the way to sort this. But I was determined to find a way to help him.

As the dark nights set in, and leaves fell from the trees, I still hadn't come up with anything. Amos was perfectly happy but I was going slowly insane!

Then he surprised me!

"I have a confession," he said over the phone.

"Oh?"

"Don't think I'm a stalker, but a while back I took some photos of you. I should have asked. Sorry... only you looked so gorgeous out there in the garden! You always do. Do you mind?"

I was so surprised — and secretly pleased.

"That's OK," I said. "Only, it's a bit unfair. You know what I look like. But I've no idea what you look like. I don't even know if you have fair hair, or dark, have blue eyes or brown..."

"I'll text you a photo," he said.

I nearly fell off the bed. "You will?"

"Give me a few minutes." He hung up.

I sat, staring at my phone. Waiting. A few minutes later it pinged.

My stomach rolled over. Finally I was going to see him.

Holding my breath, I opened up the image. The face of an angel looked back at me.

It was a close-up picture. His lovely face filled the screen, but I could see bits of blond hair. His eyes were bright blue. Perfect teeth behind a perfect smile.

My knees went weak.

More than ever I wanted to be close to him… really close!

I texted back, my fingers shaking. *Wow you are gorgeous!!!* Then hit the delete button and texted: *Nice!*

*

I couldn't wait to show Nina.

She almost fell over her own feet. "Lisa, you have to help him. It's a crime for a guy this fit to be missing out on life. What is his problem?"

"I wish I knew," I said, sadly.

That night, I couldn't sleep. It was three in the morning and I was lying in bed, listening to the rain on my windowpane, when I heard him singing.

It was a ballad. A sad ballad.

I lay there, my heart aching.

He was as lonely as me. I could tell by his voice. By the words he sang so softly.

Mine only in dreams

Apart forever it seems

You are there.

I am here.

So far apart.

Yet close in my heart.

I knew then that this wasn't a one-sided relationship. He liked me just as much as I liked him.

Who was I fooling? I didn't just *like* Amos. I was in love with him.

How insane was that?

How could I be in love with a boy I'd never even set eyes on?

Yet I was.

Dare I hope that he loved me too?

I didn't tell him I'd fallen in love with him. That was my secret. And to be honest, when we chatted, he was never sad, like I was sometimes.

But in the dead of night, when most people slept, he laid his heart bare in his songs.

I never told him that I listened to his sad songs at three and four in the morning. He might stop. And I didn't want him to stop. I could listen to his voice forever.

The thought hit me. Maybe that's all I ever would do — listen to his voice.

Never see him, never touch him.

The thought made my heart crack.

Still, I looked forward to getting home every afternoon. He would call just as I turned into our street. I guessed he watched out for me. But I never spotted him at the window, no matter how hard I looked.

We chatted about our day. For a guy who didn't go out, he always had plenty to talk about. He chatted about his online friends as if he knew them really well. As if they all hung out together.

"Have you met any of your online friends?" I asked, settling down on my bed for our usual chat.

"No, not met face-to-face," he said. "There's no need."

"Human contact!" I said.

He laughed. "Told you, I'm a computer geek. I know lots of other geeks online. Have you never heard of Nerds 'R' Us?"

"You idiot!" I laughed.

"I heard that through the wall."

"No doubt. They're paper thin…." I had a thought. For a second it seemed such a great idea. "Amos, we could make a hole in the wall. Reach through and shake hands!"

"Ha! You might peep… and I'm sure I would." His voice shook a little bit. "You're so lovely, Lisa."

I knew he wanted to be close to me. I knew it!

Desperately I begged, "Meet me, then, Amos!"

"We can't…"

"Why can't we?" I begged. "I could come to your house. I'm not asking you to go outside."

He fell silent. I held my breath, hoping he would say, *OK, come on round.*

But he said, "I'm sorry, Lisa. We can't… it would ruin everything."

"Why would it?" I cried, wanting to scream.

"I can't risk it."

"Risk what?"

"Risk losing you. I told you, friends let you down. And I think I'd die if I lost you now. You mean so much to me."

My heart lurched. Tears swam in my eyes. "Amos, you won't lose me, ever. I promise!"

"Don't make promises you can't keep, Lisa."

I was on my knees, facing the wall, facing him.

"Then tell me what's wrong with you! Why would I stop being your friend if I saw you?"

"Lisa, please, don't ask. Let's just carry on as we are. Phone buddies. Pen friends."

"I don't want a pen friend!" I wailed, thumping the wall with my fist. "I want a boyfriend!"

Tears streamed down my cheeks.

"I'm sorry," he said softly. "I'm so sorry. This isn't fair on you."

The line went dead.

CHAPTER 5
GOING CRAZY

The silence between us went on for a week.

To begin with, after he'd hung up, I just stared and stared at my phone. Expecting him to call back. But the awful silence went on and on. Hours, days. No word from him. I imagined him sitting on his bed staring at his phone, willing it to ring. Hoping I would ring him.

But his last words echoed in my head. *This isn't fair on you....*

It drove me mad. Every two minutes I was checking my phone, looking for texts or missed calls. Checking my emails.

Nothing.

Nina said it was for the best.

"He's doing you a favour, Lisa. He can't be the boyfriend you want, for whatever reason. So he's ended it. He's setting you free."

My heart ached. I didn't want to be set free. And I was worried about Amos. He'd said he'd die if our friendship ended. Was he sad? Was his heart breaking too?

After eight days of silence, walking home from school, I made up my mind. Having him as a phone buddy was better than not having him in my life at all.

I had to call him.

My heart hammered and my fingers shook as I dialled his number.

He picked up right away. "Lisa!" The word came out as a sigh. As if he'd been holding his breath all this time.

My voice shook. "Amos... how... how are you?"

"Missing you like crazy."

My heart lurched. "Same here."

"I'm sorry I hung up on you like I did, Lisa. It broke my heart to do that. But I can't be what you want. And it wasn't fair to keep saying no to you. To keep hurting you."

I'd made up my mind. Hopefully, I asked, "But we can still be phone buddies, pen friends?"

"If you're happy with that. I'm so sorry I can't give you more."

"That's OK," I said, wishing I meant it.

Deep inside I knew I would never give up hope of seeing him face-to-face. Never!

"Don't cut yourself off from other boys though, Lisa. A lovely girl like you should have a real boyfriend. Not a weirdo geek like me."

The idea of falling for anyone else was crazy. But I said OK.

We were back on track, and I was happy again. And so was Amos.

Later that week I bumped into his mum in the street. She was so normal. She smiled, said hello and went to walk on.

I called after her. Blurted out, "Why won't Amos see anyone?"

She stopped.

"Why won't he let me see him? Is it a phobia?"

She looked so sad — sad for me. "My son is not like other boys."

"I know that. But I really… care about him."

"People do care, until they see him. And then…." Her voice trailed away. "He's been hurt so many times, Lisa."

"But he can trust me!"

She took my hand. "Lisa, he won't risk that. I think, my dear, that he's in love with you."

"Oh!" My heart soared.

"And if you turned away from him, like so many so-called friends have, I fear it would destroy him."

I clung onto her hand. "I'll *never* do that! I promise!"

She smiled that sad smile. "I'll tell him. But really, Lisa, far better that you accept his way of life. Don't try to change things. People get hurt when that happens."

He didn't call me that evening. I guessed he was busy on his laptop. He'd built one website, and was starting on another. He got so wrapped up in his work, time flew for him. So finally I dialled his number.

"Hi, Lisa. Good timing!"

As always, my toes tingled at the sound of his voice. "Really, why?"

"I've been writing a song. Just finished it. I'll put my phone on speaker, but you'll hear it through the wall anyway," he laughed.

"Fantastic!"

"Hang on…."

I waited, sitting close to the wall that divided us.

He played the piano first. The loveliest of tunes. A ballad. And then he sang. Not softly as he did at three in the morning. Now his voice was crystal clear. A beautiful sound. The words echoed around my room, thrilling my heart.

Words of love. The song told of his love for a girl who he would never hold in his arms. But held her close in his heart.

My heart swelled with love for him.

When he had finished, and the final note of the piano had faded away, I could barely speak.

"Beautiful!" I said, my voice trembling. "So beautiful."

"Shall I tell you what I've called the song?" he asked.

"Yes," I said.

"'Lisa'."

I didn't get it at first, and I said, "Yes?"

He laughed. "No, it's called 'Lisa'! I've written it for you."

My eyes closed, as I tried to hold back the tears. But they flooded down my cheeks.

"You're not crying, are you?" he asked.

"Yes… but in a happy way!" It was a lie. This was breaking my heart.

Being apart was so wrong.

"So you liked it?"

"Loved it…. Oh, Amos. I know I keep asking. I know you say we can't… but we need to overcome this. You need to trust me." I took a deep breath. "Amos, I love you. I promise that if we meet, I will still love you. I will always love you!"

"You won't!" His voice broke. "Lisa, you won't!"

"I will! I promise!"

He fell silent. For a long time, he didn't say a word. I looked at my phone, in case he'd hung up again. But he was still there. I could hear him breathing.

I held my breath.

Finally, he said, "Promise me? Promise you won't hate me? You won't run away screaming?"

I shook my head. "Amos, don't be crazy."

"So promise me. Promise me that, Lisa!"

"I promise," I said, my heart soaring.

"OK," he said softly. So softly that I could barely hear him.

I closed my eyes. At last, at long last, I was going to see the boy I loved.

CHAPTER 6
BROKEN PROMISES

We made plans.

Tomorrow night, midnight, we'd meet in his garden. He would leave the gate open for me. He said he'd feel happier if it was dark. If no one else was around.

I was too excited to sleep. And couldn't wait to tell Nina.

She wasn't as over the moon as me. "Have you never heard the saying, *curiosity killed the cat?*"

"Yes, but this isn't like that! We love each other. We should be together." I was too excited to let her concerns worry me.

"Lisa, he told you he's odd," Nina went on. "You've heard how people react when they see him. But you've begged and begged until you've worn him down."

I smiled. "Yes, finally!"

She looked worried. "I just hope you don't regret it."

I told Mum and Dad what was happening. Oddly, they said the same as Nina. I ignored them. They had no idea what it was like for me. I *had* to see Amos.

I took ages getting ready that night. My hair shone, my face glowed. Best jeans, my favourite pale blue fluffy jumper. Make-up done to perfection.

I wondered if he was as excited as me. Was he in the shower, making sure he smelled good? Wondering what to wear?

The time ticked by so slowly. And then, just a few minutes to midnight, my phone rang.

Amos.

"Hi!" I said, so happy I could burst. "Are you there already? I'm just on my way."

"Lisa, I'm sorry…."

I stopped dead. "What?"

"I can't go through with this."

"Amos, no!" I screamed.

"I'm so sorry, Lisa. I'm so scared that you won't want me if we meet. I can't risk losing you forever. I can't!"

"You won't!" I cried. "I promise! Amos, I promise…."

"Friends break promises…" he whispered.

He couldn't do this. I couldn't bear it.

Frantically, I threw my phone on the bed. Flung my bedroom door open. Ran down the stairs and out of the front door. I raced around to his house. Banged my fists against his front door. Pressed my thumb on his doorbell. Yelled through the letterbox. Yelled and screamed and banged the door until my hands hurt.

I heard my parents shouting for me to come in. To stop making a scene.

I kept on yelling and thumping the door.

Finally, it opened. His mum and dad stood there.

I barged past them. Raced up the stairs.

Their house was the same layout as ours.

I knew which was Amos's bedroom.

I barged in.

In a mad flurry of arms and legs, I glimpsed Amos diving under his duvet. Dragging it around him, so he was a big hump on the bed.

"Amos, don't hide from me, please!"

"Go away, Lisa. Please go away!" screamed Amos.

I knew his parents and mine stood behind me in the doorway. His mum took my arm. "Please, Lisa, don't do this to him."

I shook her hand off me. "Amos, trust me. I won't hate you."

"You will! You'll run away screaming. Like everyone else. I don't want to lose you, Lisa."

"I won't run away screaming. I promise…
I promise…."

It was as if time stood still then. My promises just hung in the air. I held my breath. It felt like everyone was holding their breath. The silence, the stillness went on and on.

And then, very slowly, the hump of duvet began to move. Amos's arms and legs untangled themselves from the bed cover.

I stared as he came from under it, aware of my head starting to ache as a frown gathered over my eyes.

I couldn't work this out.

His arms were where his legs ought to be. His legs were where his arms should be. There was a lump of pink flesh where his head should be. It was like some monster from a horror film standing there before me. *Standing?* Did I say *standing?*

His arms and hands supported him. His legs stuck out from his shoulders.

I felt the scream start in the pit of my stomach. Rising into my throat, choking me.

Where was Amos?

Where was the lovely boy who made me laugh? The boy with the beautiful voice? The wonderful person who wrote songs that brought tears of joy to my eyes? Where was he? This wasn't him. This was some dreadful, awful, freak of nature.

He'd lied. There was no blue-eyed boy. He'd tricked me.

But then, using his toes, as he was standing on his hands, he opened his shirt and that lovely face appeared. Blue eyes wide with hope and fear, looked out from his chest.

My hopes, my dreams, all exploded in misery.

I turned away from him. How could I love this… this monstrosity?

I pushed aside everyone standing in the doorway. Stumbling down the stairs as Amos's agonised voice cried out after me.

"You promised, Lisa… you promised you wouldn't run from me. You promised…." Amos screamed.

Even with my hands clasped over my ears I could still hear him. Every cry, every sob as his heart broke.

As my heart broke.

"Lisa… Lisa, please!"

The blackness of the night engulfed me. As black and bleak and empty as my life. And I ran, blinded by tears. I ran and ran and ran….

THE END

ABOUT THE AUTHOR

Ann Evans lives in Coventry in the West Midlands. She has written over 30 books, including the award-winning *The Beast*. One of her most recent titles is *Celeste*, a time slip thriller set in her home city. Her Teen Reads and Dark Reads titles are *Nightmare*, *By My Side*, *Red Handed*, *Straw Men*, *Kicked Into Touch* and *Living The Lie*. Ann also writes magazine articles on all kinds of topics, and adult romance and crime novels.